SUN STEP BLACK LAKE

John Welson (Born 1953, Llanfair-Llythynwg, Wales) is a painter, poet, and writer. He began painting at the age of 12 having been inspired by a chance encounter with a book on Surrealism, and has since had over 350 exhibitions around the world since 1974. John has exhibited with artists as diverse as Picasso, Dali, Man Ray, Matta, Max Ernst, Grayson Perry, and Damien Hirst. His paintings are inspired by the desolate, magnetic and pulsating landscapes/ inscapes of Mid Wales.

Allan Graubard is a poet, playwright, literary critic, and curator of art. His works are translated in numerous languages and his plays have premiered in the U.S. and EU. Recent poetry and fiction include: *Western Terrace* (Exstasis Editions, Victoria, BC, 2020), *Language of Birds* (Anon Editions, NYC/LA, 2020), *A Crescent by Any Other Name* (Anon Editions, NYC/LA, 2017), *Targets* (Anon Editions, NYC/LA, 2015), *And tell tulip the summer* (Quattro Books, Toronto, 2011), *Roma Amor* (Spuyten Duyvil Press, NYC, 2009), and others.

ISBN: 978-1-915760-58-6

Cover image: 'Breeze, Summer' by John Welson

Cover designed by Aaron Kent

Edited and Typeset by Aaron Kent

Broken Sleep Books Ltd
Rhydwen
Talgarreg
Ceredigion
SA44 4HB

Broken Sleep Books Ltd
Fair View
St Georges Road
Cornwall
PL26 7YH

Sun Step Black Lake

Allan Graubard & John Welson

Broken Sleep Books

Contents

'The play's the thing…'   7

Above Black Lake   9

Colfa   13

Gift to Nature   19

Nature's Slumber – Nature Morte   29

Heather Spring   31

Spring Mist Dawn   35

Sunshine Bridge to Dusk   37

Woodland Forest Step   41

Sunrise Stone Circle   43

About the Artist   47

About the Writer   48

'The play's the thing...'

Playing is an art that individual creators mine as much for content as form. When the game involves two, in this case artist John Welson and writer Allan Graubard, and reciprocation leads and conducts, the qualities that emerge often reveal issues and experiences of a personal and collective nature; sometimes more of one, sometimes less of another, sometimes pregnant with both.

The rules of the game yet are simple, rooted in a sense of freedom and openness, with discovery the prize. Just what is it in this image and the title attached to it that prompts a written response? Just what is it in this written response that prompts an image? And how, as an ensemble, does it all live?

It is, for the artist and writer, a give and take over a period of time that enriches as it extenuates. In this game, John created his images prior to the writing but also offered an image in response to the writing received. Allan explored the images John sent to him quickly, focusing most on their titles and what they drew to them: the words and phrases that propelled the texts in this book.

Here, then, by duet, is an analog to the environments that surround us, in which we live, which live in us, and which inform and shape us. It is, as theater, a kind of conjuration, but on a printed stage, done in the spirit of play...

John Welson, *Black Lake*. Acrylic on paper. 26 x 18cm. 2019

Above Black Lake

Perhaps she is sitting somewhere
Perhaps she is wearing a heavy felt hat
Perhaps she is not there at all,
    she is not at all what we think she is
Perhaps not knowing her is better than knowing her
    or knowing her too well
Perhaps that's why she comes to this town... no, this hamlet where neighbors
    know each other by name, though it ends there
Perhaps where she can't
Perhaps with the first letter of her name, she begins... or ends... or both
    not being what she began with. This letter, so common it is, I don't recall it
Perhaps she's dressed for winter or spring. Not summer
Perhaps she prefers the cold wind she drinks down when it whips up around her
Perhaps she is an image left on a still black lake high up near the moon, or high
    up enough to take it like that high above Black Lake. Isn't that the name.
    Isn't that first letter the first letter of her name
Perhaps she's not there and we aren't. Just there, standing on a slope that
    swerves down through firs to the bank of the lake, that deep dark lake
    where light perishes soundlessly
Perhaps she's come back because she wants to, because once, here, she had an
    affair. Isn't that right? Isn't that what she wants? The sound that moves her?
    Isn't that the music in the movement that moves her?
Perhaps that's it
Perhaps that's what she thinks and feels standing on the slope that swerves to
    the bank
Perhaps she's trying not to cry
Perhaps she'd rather laugh

It's too much, too little, too quick or slow

It lingers. The affair

Perhaps she doesn't want to remember all that much about it

Perhaps she's tried to and can't

Perhaps the less it matters, the more she wants it

Perhaps she says it just like that on the slope that swerves through the firs,
bushes, dead soggy branches, rabbit or deer spunk, those old branches
covered with green lichen red lichen yellow lichen, the muddy bank where
the tide laps and the sparrows dip down to sip the rich black onyx water

Perhaps, she sees herself in the water when she gets down to it

Perhaps when she gets down to it. She sees her face and doesn't recognize it

Perhaps the game she plays at Black Lake, the rich onyx water, the heavy girth
of it swelling and rising and falling, imperceptibly, impishly, derisively...

Perhaps her felt hat, her straw hat, her sitting somewhere, her wool skirt,
her cotton skirt, her mouth just slightly open, her hands in her lap, her
eyes, her black onyx eyes, this deep dark girth on the slope above the bank
when sparrows dip their heads to sip the rich water with their beaks

Perhaps you remember her

Perhaps I don't or can't however much I want to

Perhaps relieved by the simplicity and beauty of the lake, the firs,
the girth of it swelling and falling

Perhaps that's all she wants or doesn't want to admit she wants in that way, at
the bank bending down, cupping water in her two hands and sipping

John Welson, *Colfa*. Acrylic on paper. 78cm x 59cm. 2011

Colfa

They told me that, when I reached Colfa, however 'picaresque' it was – they used that word, unexpected it was, too — from the 17th century but with a history far back, perhaps to the end of the last Ice Age, I should avoid it. If I couldn't and an overnight was all I needed, then the guest house on Cistercian Street was a good bet; if, that is, it was open. But stay no longer than a night...

Six years later to the day, March 4, 2029, I am still here. Was there any other place? In that other time before I met her — in a dream – yes, that first night...

Several weeks prior, while in London, I realized that I could chart a walk in Wales. A solo camino with the coast – no particular place, just that I reached the sea; those waves, crashing onto a beach, the steel grey with white caps and gulls searching for prey and the wind and wet... I am drawn to it: the Atlantic, Pacific, the Adriatic, Aegean, Mediterranean, Gulf of Mexico – place names to a composite passion in which and by which I've lived...

I'm not certain now... if... Hell, it doesn't matter...

I packed what I needed, a few changes of clothing, flashlight, compass, cell phone, recharger, toiletries – the basics – what you think you know you need...

Two weeks to reach the coast. Eight or ten miles a day. And hope the weather held out its warm kind hand. I'd eat and bed where I could. I'd read somewhere that the walking route I'd outlined – rural roads mostly – usually led to a village or hamlet, and if there wasn't a hotel or guest house the locals would open their homes up for a modest fee...

And so they did. Once only did I sleep in a field... rimmed by Oaks and Sycamores, it was... just too tired, the dusk deepening into darker inky striations... I found a patch of dried moss on a low hill, unrolled my sleeping bag, ate and drank what I'd brought along – bread, cheese, olives, figs, two thick slices of ham and water – pissed a ways off, then crawled in and went out quick...

I woke near dawn, the blue lightening, the birds going at it... and set off again, happy to have done what I did... sleeping on dried moss...

It's stayed with me, the strength and devil may care... I'll prompt what I get... enough or more than enough or less than more than I wanted or expected or found...

Colfa, and the warning or caution that a farmer and his wife offered, so generous and hospitable... traipsing up to their home, nothing else around, and offering to pay... if they had an extra room to sleep in or a bed anywhere else and supper... there was an unused bedroom and hot water for a bath... I needed a bath... but be careful with the hot water... it scalds... and we have no way to control it...

That night I had this dream.

Midwinter, snowy midnight. The Black Forest. I was seated in an antique horse-drawn equipage. The horses knew the route and stayed to it. A good thing... There was no driver. Approaching a bend – the snow had stopped – the horses slowed to a halt. I opened the door and stepped out and walked on in to the wood. That's just the way it was in the dream. I walked through that wood enticed by the fresh clear air which stung the deeper I took it in, the snow with its thin top skin of ice, when too high or heavy falling off the boughs with a crack, the caw of a crow or raven, the frigid sparkling clarity of it all...

And I kept on until I didn't know where I was or if I could find my way back to that equipage or what it might mean if I did or didn't. And if I stopped and sank down, leaning against a tree trunk and nodded off? What if it snowed again? What then...?

The questions came and went... The counterpoint?... I'd be better off inside rather than outside. At least I knew that, crunching slowly through the snow, the white sucking weight of it...

Then a yellow light flickering through dark thick trunks, the distant acrid scent of burning wood... I dragged to that cottage with its peaked thatch roof, some cliché of a peasant's cottage I'd come across... and knocked...

The old door creaked open. A frail, stooped white-bearded man looked me over then stood aside...

'What we have, you have' he said, as I entered. 'It won't be much, but it suits us and it's warm.'

I knew that old man. I'd seen him before. Then a name came: Robert Frost.

Before a large, uneven stone fireplace, a young woman in a green dress stirred a deep coal-black pot. Auburn hair fell to her shoulders. Aquiline face finely set eyes and thanks, even for a stranger, in their home, there, with them...

'We haven't eaten.' Frost said, motioning to a rough-hewn table.

The three of us sat down to a stew: rabbit and lamb and wild vegetables and spices they'd gathered and dried out when autumn was theirs and the cold hadn't come. A pitcher of milk from the cow that morning. That's what we drank and we chatted... who they were... where I'd come from... what I was doing alone in that forest at night...

Several days later, in Colfa, while at the open air market searching for a bottle of moonshine – so struck was I by the poignancy of the dream that I stuck around – I saw her or a woman so much like her that I couldn't tell the difference. Tall, shapely, auburn hair falling to her shoulders, a green dress – *that dress.* She swapped tales with a vegetable vendor about her age; apparently they knew each other. When she finished and saw me gazing at her, she blushed and turned away. But that brief exchange was enough...

She lived here, was born here, and taught at the local school. Oh, she'd been to cities, graduated from university and after some travel round about, as young women do these days, came back to stay.

I was lonely. And she, well, hadn't she stepped out of a dream? That gushy, all too hopeful song that men, men usually, cozen up to, whether they want to or not. Choice in such matters being something you just don't have.

Foolish was it to think we could or might find in each other what we missed in ourselves? And, having found it, not let it go? It's easy to criticize a fool or a foolish decision made in the heat of the moment. But when it happens and two take to it, fools times two is an equation that lives on its merits.

Nor are those merits mine. They aren't. They're ours. Two fools together in Colfa... In or because of or by way of this crusty odd hamlet I was warned against... Why? I can't say now and really don't care...

Fools times two...

John Welson, *Glascwm*. Oil on Canvas. 82x56cm. 2018

Gift to Nature

We met each other by chance on the ferry that runs between Uig on Skye to North Uist — on one of those Spring afternoons still tipped toward Winter. He was tall, clean cut, with thin tufted greying hair grey, good cheekbones and that aged lined look that men above 60 possess; men that have lived more than they show, whether they want to or not. He was standing by the railing in a weathered blue trench coat, a fedora in his hand. He looked very much like me. In fact, he could have been me if I didn't know any better; if I'd forgotten for a moment what made me *me* – and that's happened; yes, it's happened.

I don't usually start conversations with strangers, I wasn't lonely or desperate... but at least now I can sense why, if just partly, I broke in.

'Always great when you're leaving... and arriving.'

He didn't respond although he certainly heard me. Then, as if pulled from a memory or a dream that struck him deeply, he shivered – but it wasn't cold, not at all. Aware now that I had spoken, he turned toward me, accents of surprise and shame twisting through his eyes.

'What was that?' he asked.

I slowly repeated what I said as if he needed it, some casual anchor to steady himself with, and it worked.

'Have we met?'

'I don't think so. Glascwm.'

'Robert.'

He nodded, the kind of greeting you give someone you don't want to talk to, and turned back to the sea cut by the prow, quick whitecaps rolling off low waves, the wind and that brilliant sun.

Two months later.

Recalling it now, I wonder if it ever happened. And of the events that transpired after we landed, disembarked, and met again, once, at the Owl, one of three pubs on the island, have taken on such an eccentric tint that that first encounter seems of a piece but reversed – with Robert breaking the silence as I stood by the railing, lost in that receding coastline and the expansive watery vista; as if the one required the other, as if the one without the other could not exist as it did.

A week after disembarking.

I came to the island to find the kind of solitude I didn't have with my wife in town, in that comfortable, old flat we've shared now for decades. I needed to write – not that I make my living by it – and the common distractions at home were as fruit to a fly.

Of course it was only after she asked me if I'd written anything of my own other than the book reviews I was known for that I realized I hadn't for too long. So I rented a room at Penguin Inn, a cozy place on a quiet side street near that modest harbor for fishing boats mostly, and told her I'd be gone for a while and that if she wanted to join me to come in a week.

She walked over, took my face in her hands and kissed me.

'No, school starts soon enough. I have to prepare the syllabus and we need a break from the daily grind. Enjoy yourself and get something down on paper you can develop. I know how you work.'

On the sixth day, a Monday, I'd finally gotten into it, a tale took hold of me and wouldn't let go. I write in fits and starts, never sure of where I'm heading, sensitive at least to the moment, the scratch of the pen on paper – I don't write on screen, just too facile. In any event, writing is as much psychological as it is physical, however you look at it, and grasping a pen is an inducement.

And while I still had a ways to go, sketching out from the mist a singular route, I knew I'd laid a foundation to 'develop,' as she so kindly put it. I can't tell you how many tales I couldn't develop; tales that fell by the wayside; odd flutterings blown this way and that until they took their last breath and dropped away.

'Enough,' I muttered. I pushed the chair back from the small desk in the room, stood up, glanced outside to see if the wind was blowing hard as it tended to by late afternoon – it wasn't – slipped into a light jacket, took the key and my wallet and left.

Now Lochmaddy isn't a town I'd ever boast about but it does serve its purpose. It hosts, and has hosted for centuries, a population dedicated to the sea, fishing first but now with some summer tourists who enjoy its spare qualities, sports fishing included. In that open glittering sea big fish roam. There's a lovely beach in a nearby cove that's good for swimming by July, which also draws young families from the mainland looking for a cheap getaway. Couples use the town for a quick escape, too. Beyond that and the two churches, three pubs, the daily seafood and vegetable market set up in the morning under tarpaulins at the harbor until the vendors sell out or call it a day, a town hall aptly named 'Druid's Hall' scrawled in fine wood script above the front door lintel where locals hold court deciding on what and how with infrastructure and other necessities, and one larger retail joint for provisions – from meat and eggs to heating oil, generators, saws, nails, paint – that's it. Have I forgotten the school, built in the 30s, which serves students from elementary through high school, with a cafeteria that seconds for a film and dramatic theater and the public library attached to it? I suppose I have.

The seaward side of the island spots several dairy farms, set in low valleys, until the escarpment rises to rocky cliffs where gulls and the odd albatross nest, waves rumbling in below and crashing with great spumes of spray. The view there is terrific if that's what gets you. And there's an ancient neolithic rock circle open to the elements to wonder at why here, and what it was that drove them, the ancestors, to get just those boulders in that alignment to do what they did in it and for it.

I loved it all. Perhaps because that's how I'm made, a city boy happy enough to be away from the rough and tumble. Perhaps because being away from my wife sharpened my hunger for her – another reason why I came. Perhaps because I can't do without being transient for as long as I want it and can take it.

I walked over to the Owl, the nearest pub, a 19th century affair, as I learned, built on an older pub that had burnt to the ground from a lightning strike. Pushed open the door and stepped up to the bar.

Cocktail hour is a tradition I've celebrated since I came of age and could buy liquor. Not only does it mark a transition – the day trailing into dusk – it also signals an ending, with work the victim.

The bartender, John by name, was a spry fiftyish born on the island. He'd left for the merchant marine and returned to make a go of it after his parents' death. They owned and ran the pub 'forever,' as he tells it to whomever asks. And more than a few do, locals included, if only to hear him say it again with that lilt that makes the word an entrée into a private world without beginning or end, or so he makes it seem; a kind of seeming that just warms you up, yes, to order.

Oddly, the place was empty.

'Afternoon. Scotch; a double, with water to chase.'

The amber liquid when drunk in excess induces a stupor I've never enjoyed, despite having done that more than enough. But when drunk in modest amounts, its therapeutic qualities take over – heightening sensation, mollifying stress and in the right circumstances enhancing desire though I wasn't here for that. There's something else, too, about holding a glass of scotch in hand. When lifting it up and gazing through it, pondering the events that brought me here, it revives a predilection for prophesy, almost as crystal gazing does. In the glass form shapes and suggestions of events past and future; the things that have happened and what will happen. And however briefly they appear in this miniature amber sea as it swirls and vibrates, I sense them, dimly or clearly. Then, but only then, I bring the glass to my lips, hold it there and sip.

The door opened.

Footsteps.

Robert chose a stool beside me separated by another stool.

'Scotch?'

'Yes,'

'I'll have the same.' Then raising his voice, 'I'll have the same.'

When the drink came, he lifted the glass and gazed into it, tilting it slightly this way and that. An elixir it was. And while I did not know if he used it as I did, our taste for scotch bridged the difference.

'We met on the ferry – last week.'

He glanced at me as he set the glass down.

'Yes.'

'Been here before?'

'A few times. You?'

'The same.'

Silence.

We sipped.

Then, not wanting to pry but being the only two at the bar, I asked him this, slowly and attentively.

'What brings you here?'

Silence again.

One minute stretched into two.

'Nothing... in particular.'

Was it the finality in his response that startled me, that first word and second phrase breaking apart without recourse, or his lifting the glass, jutting his head back a notch and downing what was left?

He placed the glass on the bar as if it meant something and stood up, the stool clattering back. He tipped his head in recognition, turned around and walked out.

John, who'd busied himself with drying dishes at the far end of the bar, but I'm sure who took it all in, came over, glanced quizzically at the door, shrugged and asked if I wanted another.

'Yes, thanks,' I responded.

There was something familiar about Robert, something intimate, his terseness notwithstanding. Who was he? What did he do on the mainland? Why with the bar empty did he sit close enough, so that we could, if we wanted to, talk about anything at all if only to find in the exchange enough to satisfy our need for rapport, however pissant or poignant it was?

I still can't say. But that moment silently, secretly bore into me.

I hung out at the bar for another half an hour until the regulars came in, finished at last with work or whatever it was that filled up their day. The routine was a release, and the more so since they knew each other; citizens each of the island that kept and fed and taught them how to live as they did, as they could afford, and for a few a bit more than that.

Then in some charade of mimicry, as clear as it was funny, I threw my head back, downed the last of the drink, placed the glass on the bar and a bill large enough to cover Robert's drink, he hadn't paid, pushed the stool back and walked out.

In itself the sequence was not unusual. Anyone at the bar might have done the same. But infused by a sense of repetition, which mimicry makes use of – sometimes mixed with envy, other times mockery – a smile formed, slight yet pointed.

Now I don't place much trust or interest in dreams. I dream like you dream. Rarely remember them when waking up. But this one that night was different.

And when I think about it so many months later, I'm as much surprised that I can recall it as by its effect, which still shakes me.

Was this one of those dreams that crosses the border between nocturnal and diurnal? Did it, as most all of my dreams do not, infect my awareness enough to wonder what was, what is more real?

Despite my opacity here, the innumerable dreams that sink away into morning and which, at best, I can recall fragments of, this dream remains.

It went like this.

On the ferry that runs between Uig on Skye and North Uist — it was one of those Spring afternoons still tipped toward Winter — there was a tall, older guy at the railing, gazing at the receding coast. He didn't notice me as I came up and took in the that watery vista. We stood like that, the two of us, until I mentioned how great it was to leave the coast and land somewhere else; the simple joy of transit, of departing and arriving. He heard me but didn't respond. When he did, half turning, hands clutching the railing, surprise and shame twisted through his eyes. Something was up. The guy had seen what I hadn't and while he wouldn't admit or acknowledge it, the stakes intensified – *for me.* And the dream took on a sudden heaviness. It was as if that guy on that ferry and that vista held an unwanted, unbidden and uncertain immanence.

Had I begun to dream as he did? Had his vision become mine? Perhaps. But whether or not it was true in the dream, the possibility, no, the probability of it, *shakes me.*

Dreams are episodic. Scenes rise and evaporate and other scenes take their place. Rarely do dreams evolve in a clear, linear line.

I was in a large Gothic chateau with high-arched ceilings, dim lamplight, and a sense of pressure from above that thickened the overall penumbral tone. Other than the distant sound of rushing water – the sea the ferry crossed turned into a sloped river pouring into that sea – silence reigned.

I turned to a low table in the center of the room, either which I'd missed when entering the room or which did not yet exist. On it sat the head of a bull. It's bulging eyes had yellowed and gluey, glistening petrified slaver slung from the corners of its lips. Dull curdles of black blood gathered at its base, where a butcher had carelessly made the jagged cut.

The thing appalled, disgusted and captivated me. I drew closer to it until I bumped against the table. I bent down to the monstrance, its thick stiff tongue stretched out over busted teeth; a last useless reflex before the end.

Would the interchange about to occur, which I sensed was about to occur, and which I could not prevent, happen? Would *it* replace my head and my head replace *it*, there on that broad low table in that vaulted Gothic room in a chateau at the end of the world, the world I knew and loved and didn't want to leave ever? Would I see through those pitiless eyes? Would it taste with a tongue suddenly warm and voracious?

The scream in a nightmare is the moan of a man asleep. It is also the means a man needs to wake up. As the scream intensifies, the moan deepens. The man struggles, spasmodic, until the eyes crack open. Then and only then does the anguish deflate and the trauma subside.

Was it that, that decapitated bull's head that held him when I approached; a dream, day dream or hallucination, call it what you will, that he had at that railing on that ferry, and which after meeting him again at the pub became a chateau dressed up in Gothic darkness and gore?

The damn thing gets me. Nor is figuring it out the point. Sometimes between two people an interchange makes something happen, awake, asleep or both. And that's the full of it. And, no, I didn't see Robert again. Perhaps he left the island. I stayed on for another week and finished what I'd started. This very tale you're holding between your hands or staring at on screen. I didn't know it when I began it but I was simply writing what was happening. But isn't that what makes a tale stick, with a savage, shared dream as an ender? If not, then forgive me and go back to what you were doing – if you can do it as you were doing it before you began to read this, wondering just what you were reading and why.

John Welson, *Nature's Slumber*. Acrylic on paper. 74x48cm. 2019.

Nature's Slumber – *Nature Morte*

When a man flips a coin into a placid fountain on a warm Spring afternoon without making a wish or, for that matter, understanding what he didn't do, marking him as just another tourist in the city he lives in, *that man* begins to evaporate from the head down — as if he were little more than a drink gone flat. And if that man, dressed for business, his business, whatever that is, accustomed, as he is, to rarely admitting anything of value – his standing, for instance, across multiple positions, from banal to incendiary – though in this instance the latter is quite far-fetched – then he, just before disappearing entirely, will leave, as if saying good-bye, a token without which we, his audience, are lost, incapable of knowing or intuiting more about him than these poor words reveal.

But this is in the tradition we, you and I, celebrate, even without intending to. It comes from a once calibrated artistic etiquette that war has eviscerated; our endless pean to mechanized slaughter, which compels and disgusts us, attracting and distracting us from the moment that cognizance, lost to sleep, emerges with dawn; the distant thud of canon underlining, again, just how precarious it is to be here, just several feet from that man who reached into his pocket for a coin and flipped it into the fountain with all the nonchalant conviction of an amnesiac.

God be praised that he won't remember the gesture or if he does, won't be able to say why he did it.

'Nature's Slumber,' exiled to this imbroglio, is just as facile. Is what he lost, though, our gain? Or will he, in leaving his token, that coin sinking to the bottom of the fountain, return, perpetually modest, insensibly opaque, ever resurrected on the right side of a torn, scumbled portrait painted with a scavenger's brush; a portrait blown askew on a burned, half-destroyed wall in a gallery on the city's north side where bombs fall and bloody anguish blooms...?

John Welson, *Heather Spring*. Crayon on paper. 85x61cm. 2010

Heather Spring

The Spring sits on top of an old washing machine in the junk yard. A tightly wound metal screw strung with heather. Someone left it there. Someone wound that heather on that spring. Someone was crazy enough or stupid enough to do that. To spend the time it takes to do that. Then leave it there and forget about it. That's the size of it. A few inches long, it is. I once dreamed it was longer. Maybe a foot. Maybe longer. Dreams don't lie. My mother told me that. I was young. Now I'm old. But I remember her telling me that. What she didn't say is what I learned later on. Life does. Lie. Dreams don't but life does. A tango. Better yet a waltz. Me and you. Trapsing around the living room. Waiting for that heavenly moment. I'm not religious, very religious, you know. Spring wound with heather. I didn't do that but I wanted to do that. I left it on the washing machine. That burnt out rusted tilted lichened machine. Just enough so that the tilt makes it seem as if it's about to fall. How long before the little slope it's leaning on washes away or blows away? Nothing to hold it up. And the heather spring will roll off it into the mud or the dust. That odd little spring wound with heather by someone thoughtful enough to do that. I guess there's as much reason to that as there isn't reason at all. I guess that's the way of things nowadays. It's there all right. Holding it in my hands. I didn't do that but I wanted to. And somehow, some time I will. Hold it in my hands. Soft heather dried out is much like any other weed when it dries out. Stiff, crumbly, useless, inane it is. Not stupid, mind you. Not that bad. Just... inane. In a name. (laughing). In name. Wonderful, isn't it, how words become other words. How one comes from the other. One in the other. What do they call that? Chinese boxes? One box then a smaller box in that box and a smaller box in that smaller box and another smaller box and so on, smaller and smaller and smaller until there's nothing left to see.

But it's there. On the washing machine. It's not in a box either. It's sitting there. So useless. And so intriguing. That heather spring. Leather sing. Lulu la la. La la la la laaaaaa. Ah, that was good. That song. Well, not a song really but like a song. A little bitsy song. Moves me. Always has. When I sing it moves me. Even if it's just a trifle, a few musical words. A little salt to spice it up. Some red pepper, too. Damn that stuff makes me sneeze. Red pepper, you know. Have to be careful with red pepper and heather springs and washing machines and sunlight. Yes, of course. The light to see the washing machine and the heather spring. When it's dark, where is it? What is it? Who cares about it? Why does anyone care about it when they can't see it at night? Moonlight? Never enough. Starlight? You've got to be kidding. But with the sun, it all changes. Wonderful. The light, the first of it, wan, thin, breathless, inching on. But it's there. Then more of it, wan to yellow, that gray yellow. Then just light. Ah, there it is! I thought I lost you. I thought... No. Stop thinking. That's what he told me. Stop thinking about it. Just do it. I'm doing it, aren't I? I'm doing it, almost done with it. That little heather spun spring in the sunlight on the old fetid, infested washing machine. Right now I am conjuring a washing machine. I see it. I sense it, right there, in the junk yard. My junk, too. The front junk yard. The back junk yard. Piles of junk. Dented hubcaps, busted window frames, termite eaten support wood, flip up phones, distressed chairs and couches and douches. Oh, forgive me. I didn't mean that. A woman douches. Men don't. They do. We don't. Myriads of stuff from another world back then when yards were grass, not junk. Not a washing machine tiled precariously with a heather spring on its top. Staying in place. Now that's something. How in the hell can it stay in place when the damn thing tilts precariously? I just don't know. What to say about it any longer. There. Heather spring. I've said it. Wonderful sound. The aspirant, the conjugant, the vowel, the consonant. The treasure trove of a diminutive world defined by the heather wound onto it. Because someone did that. Took the time it takes to do that, making something new and having the time to enjoy it, however silly it seems now. Then it was. Now it is, if a little less, a lot more less, a lot lot less than what it was when that person, the girl, that boy, that girlboy, boygirl, wound heather around the spring and dreamed of water, warmth, ripples, frogs, minnows, jays, sparrows, egrets, turkeys, chickens come to sip from the spring wild with heathery banks, swaying from the soft mud up to the top of their pink purple red blue brush flowers. Ahh, heather and springs and the air warm and welcoming... even here... in a junk yard... with that corroded, tilted, flea bag washing machine.

John Welson, *Spring Mist Dawn*. Acrylic on paper. 26x16cm. 2023

Spring Mist Dawn

I have for several days now struggled to come to terms with my inability to sketch even briefly the vast implications that three words compel: *spring mist dawn*. Even their minutiae escape me in cliches that are better forgotten but which populate the very air we breathe, you and I. If I can find any solace at all, it comes because I have found a way to elude the stress of failure, this absence that falls to the pit of the stomach and which absorbs, slowly or quickly, what does it matter, the physical and emotional plateaus that hunger instills. And yet, drawn as I am to those words, become chalk white frescoed glyphs floating in the bluing sky – a simple image, yes, but finally an image – I listen to the music they hold within them: the hard 'g,' the near onomatopoetic sibilance that dovetails to the percussive 't,' and the final diminuendo that slightly opens its lips to whisper an end note. And from that score aerial missives strip down to their vegetal bones and silver throated Gorgons in bright red skirts powder their bristled cheeks.

Music can sometimes do this where meaning cannot. The former infecting the latter until they couple, unfazed by their differences or distinctions, happy at last to have found that intemperate dance, which marks them and us, mirrors that we are to each other.

Spring mist dawn...

The trio evanesces, the words decouple, their music lingers for as long as we hear them and then, hushed, the room carries their last vibration in 'n.'

An end.

John Welson, *Sunshine Bridge to Dusk*. Acrylic on paper. 26x16cm. 2022

Sunshine Bridge to Dusk

Just west of New Orleans where the levees snake up the river – steep rising grassy slopes with a flat, narrow top that you can drive or walk on – are hamlets lost to time, more or less, and the sharp compulsions that keep us in thrall. Vagrant leftovers originally attached to old sugar cane plantations that once ruled the area, then margined out by Jim Crow because no one else wanted to live there. Black they were and are, and perhaps only now faint glimmers on a realtor's map as possible conscripts for subdivisions, they appear and vanish too quickly: a few ramshackle sun-bleached family homes, the front yards strewn with throwaways (a rusted washing machine, half of a burned out car, busted tricycles, smashed furniture), and, maybe, just maybe a lone store with essentials down that dusty road a bit.

Given the few locals who remain, who didn't have it in them to leave, or didn't have enough to leave with, and proper towns near enough with their shopping malls, how those country stores kept on adds to their mystery. Perhaps the owners found other ways to bring in some cash – drug drops, cock fighting, poker, you name it — enough at least to take care of the mortgage and property taxes, low as they are. Perhaps, with their parents having done the mortgage, they don't have much to worry about other than electricity and gas. Perhaps, not knowing what else to do or how to go about doing it, they stick around waiting for it all to come tumbling down with a contract for the land, hamlet included.

Whatever the reason, it is as if in these cast offs — whose people worked long and hard for their bosses' wealth, schooled enough to do it despite the little they made in return, and now nothing much at all — the cesura they offered, this quietus to the urban tempo, my tempo, however stifled by the wet, late afternoon summer heat, drew me in; the lure? — their low-slung, unkempt humid *presence*.

Was it all a sideshow conducted by unseen hairy claws blown up to some gigantism that the clouds hid, those heavy, darkly streaked, ominous Gulf thunderheads?

Sometimes it seemed so; sometimes it didn't.

Now some years back, when exploring the area, drawn as we were by dereliction, both objective and intimate, it was just such a moment. My wife and I, searching for ruined antebellum memorials, had discovered several long-abandoned, still standing French homes, built probably by the first cane planters to settle there two centuries ago and more. With them, of course, came that slave-infected culture we yet struggle with. The first floor, a kind of above ground basement, was of crumbling brick, moss rooting through the plaster. The second floor, all cypress, with its long, mottled, rickety porch, was still strong enough to support us. Surrounded by thick weedy swathes, they not only entombed their past but also gave to it, as if in retrospect, an incipient chorus; the cutting rasp of cicadas, buzzing wasps we'd disturbed, inconstant cawing crows and interludes of silence so rich and quick that they held us, suspended in some time that was no time but this time, empty, extensive, and useless.

Nor did it take long for it all to repel us. It's one thing to explore a ruin, another thing to sense it seeping in right through the skin, ever so slowly drowning in anonymity what we held so dear; this generous complicity that kept us together. So, after the second encounter, we were through, and sweaty enough and thirsty enough and hungry enough to find some store for a beer and sandwich.

River Road followed the levee. Soon enough, in a small empty field that backed onto a forest, there it was. I pulled up into a dirt lot before the front screen door and turned the engine off. We gazed at the dim interior and its cool promise. Were we heat stroked, dehydrated? A bit, yes. And it seemed for a moment that an oasis, however poorly it confused us, mirage or not, had risen from the light.

I told her to wait, opened the car door, crossed over and walked in.

The cashier, a bald, portly fellow and two friends or relatives, I couldn't tell which, leaned over the counter talking lowly. They glanced at me and returned to their conversation. It didn't matter who I was, what I wanted, or that I was the only customer there – a white man in a black store that served a black hamlet beset by poverty and an unforgiving margin along the levee that didn't provide much more.

There was an old red coke cooler on the floor filled with beer. It was the kind you slipped some quarters into the slot, pushed in till it clicked, pulled out, then lifted the glass door to reach down and grab a bottle or two. The slot, though, was rusted through. Otherwise, there were a few shelves stocked here and there with canned goods and packaged bread; Evangeline Maid, I think. The bread turned my stomach. But the name; that name stuck. I took two beers and looked around for a sandwich; anything, in fact, we could eat. But, no, there was nothing.

'Do you have any sandwiches?'

They glanced at me and turned away.

'A sandwich. You know, some cold cuts between two pieces of bread with mustard and mayo?'

No response.

I walked over to the cashier, carefully placed two one dollar bills flat on the counter beside him, pushed open the screen door and got into the car. I gave one beer to my wife, placed one between my legs, turned the key, backed up and drove off.

'No sandwiches. Just three guys chewing the fat. And not at all interested in a white man with money to spend and nothing to buy.'

'Oh?' she asked.

'Yeah.'

But that beer was cold and it was enough to keep us going till we found someplace else.

John Welson, *Woodland Forest Step*. Acrylic on paper. 26x16cm. 2022

Woodland Forest Step

There is no first step. One step follows another. And as they add up the woodland ends. A distant shoreline with crashing waves glitters in the gaining light. Or the silhouette of the city's spires, dark vertical rectangles, pentagrams, pyramids, parallelograms, arches and domes mark the transition; that interzone where animals gain human avidities and humans animal strength. Or height upon height receding into the distance until haze obscures them, pinnacles carved by desire and memory. The steps multiply, an exponential ascesis in whose culmination coordinates reverse — west become east, north south – then collapse; space gutting time, time drowning space and the improbable impossible sweet pulp of absence... these gyres amidst swirling seas, these salts fallen from fleece comets, these ganglions sprouting from bitter kisses outline in blue ink the shape of the foot that steps from the woodland to the next outcropping, pituitary and glamorous, massive boulders balanced on archaic dice carved from tusks of desiccated spectrums and wiry aeonic crowns of sparkling dust...

There is no first step. The journey winds, wounds, ripples, rattles, abrogates, embraces, carves, entrusts, distrusts, congeals, commingles, comforts and abuses and striates the unleavened crusts that dusk shapes in this grand microbial haven where words pullulate and arboreal shadows, supple nocturnes, irradiate consensual spindrifts and other divinatory captions carved onto ancient bathhouse walls.... *where the woodland ends...*

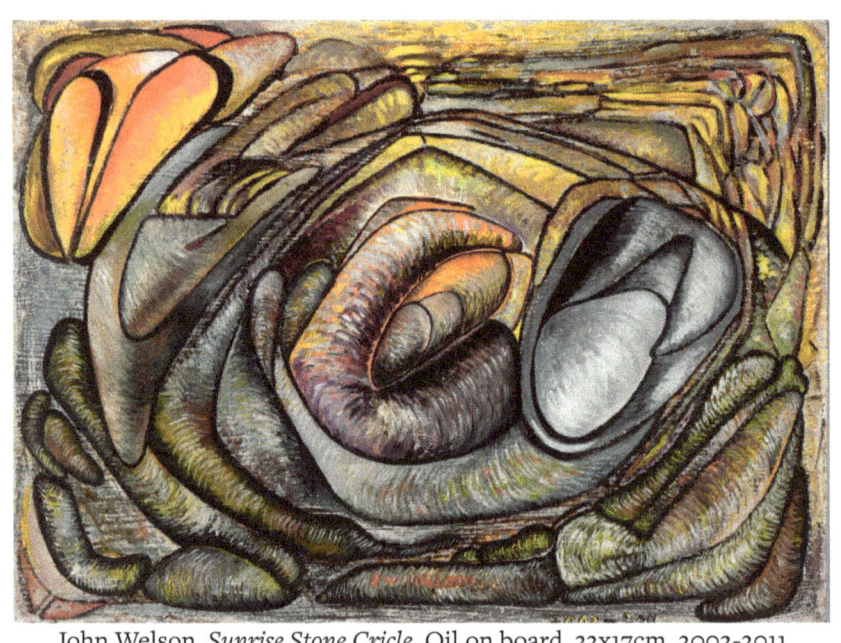

John Welson, *Sunrise Stone Cricle*. Oil on board. 32x17cm. 2002-2011

Sunrise Stone Circle

When in the early summer the sun rises over the far hill, the stone circle throws its first infant shadow. It is a moment to remember. As the thin dark line appears faintly then distinctly at the base of each stone, whether in front or behind, depending on its location, the entire circle seems to lean forward and backward. The contrapuntal animation this gives to the neolithic site on its low stubbled rise from the valley that separates it from the hill incites a curious avidity in those who have come to experience just this moment. Allied to laughter although not yet vocal – the sudden inescapably pleasant convulsions of the diaphragm that prompts the mouth to open the tongue to curl upward or downward, the lips to part and the eyes to glisten – it yet commands.

For some physiologists who have studied the phenomenon, this precursor to guffaws, its effects parallel the rhythmic pulsations that precede orgasm. And given the archeological evidence found at the site – pliable fetish-like stones crudely carved into simulacra of male and female sexual organs, oval shaped and elongated — there is reason to believe that whatever separates us from our ancestors, beyond technology, is useless conceit. The pleasures that root in visual stimulation have less to do with history as we have charted it than they do with desire and passion; a premiere characteristic of our species.

In this respect, taking the stone circle as a lens that focuses our attention on a form of autoeroticism, for even those first few minutes of dawn, is not so far-fetched. Thereafter, and I mean by that one to two minutes thereafter, with the sun having risen that much higher, grown that much brighter, the shadows that much broader, the effects begin to fade. Why this occurs is a question that neither I, a writer intrigued by the phenomenon, nor scientists who study it, can explain other than by recognizing its cause and our response to it, which age rarely tempers. Men and women in their 80s report sensations as piquant and delectable as those in their teens and 20s. The only difference tends to be its localization in the body, with the latter group enjoying its diffusion throughout the musculature while the former feels it most in the penis and vagina.

This is not to foreclose on other possible explanations that attribute the effects to less holistic or more urgent compulsions that may not be purely sexual. But there is little doubt that sexuality does intervene, however it happens, where it happens and with what intensity.

Notwithstanding the temporal aspect – those luscious few minutes during which viewers almost laugh, so close are they to primitive vocalization – with several respondents (a very small minority of the larger groups interviewed) admitting to laughing in fact, so overcome were they – it is quite clear that the circle excites us as it did those who came long before us, and which perhaps is the reason they built it to last.

All you have to do is be there as the early summer night lessens and the sunlight halos the top of that hill a half-mile or so across from the low rise where the stone circle sits. Then, as the shadows form, you can tell me how it all went, what you felt, where you felt it, and how the star that gives us life has once again made us into acolytes of its prodigious power to burn, heal and engender.

About the Artist

John William Welson, born 8th March 1953, Llanfair-Llythynwg, Sir Faesyfed, Wales, UK.

Painter, poet, writer. Lives in Wales and comes from a very long line of farmers in the mountainous area of Mid Wales. Began painting Surrealist paintings at the age of 12 years having chanced upon a book on Surrealism in the school library. Studied at Worcester and Stourbridge Colleges of Art. Over 350 exhibitions around the world. Has participated in International Surrealist activities since 1974. Met Paul Garon the Surrealist and writer on The Blues and early Blues singers in 1973. First One man exhibition, London, 1974, opened by the Surrealist Conroy Maddox. Met Vincent Bounoure (Bulletin de liaison Surrealiste), Paris, 1975, and invited to exhibit in 'Surrealist Collage' Galerie Le Triskel. Participated in 'Marvelous Freedom-Vigilance of Desire' 1976, International Surrealist Exhibition, Chicago (Franklin Rosemont). With Conroy Maddox and Paul Hammond reformed the London Surrealist Group,1977. Met Edouard Jaguer (leader of Mouvement Phases),1977, joined Mouvement Phases (showed 21 times with Phases). Had the privilage of meeting and becoming friends with the painter Jean Claude Charbonel, referred to as being 'Celtic Brothers' by Edouard Jaguer. Joint exhibition 'Surrealism-the Celtic Eye', National Library of Wales, Aberystwyth, 2011. Met Roberto Matta in 1978 and in 2011 participated in '100 Anos de Matta' in Chile, a celebration of Roberto Matta's gift and kindness. Contributed essays, poetry and illustrations to publications around the world and was included in *On the Thirteenth Stroke of Midnight, Surrealist Poetry in Britain* (edited by Michel Remy, Carcanet Press), 2013.

About the Writer

Allan Graubard is a poet, playwright, literary critic, and curator of art. His works are translated in numerous languages and his plays have premiered in the U.S. and EU. As curator, he has collaborated with museums and galleries in the US and EU; most recently, with the Eugenio F. Granell Foundation, Santiago de Compostela, Spain, for: *Dragons: The Art of Eugenio F. Granell and Rik Lina* (2022) and *Calle Cervantes: The Art of Collage by David Coulter* (2023).

Allan's poetry and fiction works include: *Western Terrace* (Exstasis Editions, Victoria, BC, 2020), *Language of Birds* (Anon Editions, NYC/LA, 2020), *A Crescent by Any Other Name* (Anon Editions, NYC/LA, 2017), *Targets* (Anon Editions, NYC/LA, 2015), *And tell tulip the summer* (Quattro Books, Toronto, 2011), *Roma Amor* (Spuyten Duyvil Press, NYC, 2009), and others.

He is the editor of and contributor to *Into the Mylar Chamber: Ira Cohen* (Fulgur, UK, 2019); advisor for and contributor to the *International Encyclopedia of Surrealism* (Bloomsbury, UK, 2019); advisor for and contributor to *The Art of Conduction,* by composer-conductor Lawrence D. 'Butch' Morris (Karma Books, NYC, 2017); advisor for and contributor to *A Phala: Revisita do Movimento Surrealista* (Sao Paolo, Brazil, 2015); guest editor of and contributor to a centennial celebration of poet Gherasim Luca (*Hyperion,* Contra Mundum Press, NYC, 2015); and, with Thom Burns, coedited and contributed to *Invisible Heads: Surrealists in North America – An Untold Story* (Anon Editions, NY/LA, 2015).

As guest writer and lecturer, he has appeared at: MoMA PS1, NYU Tisch School for the Arts, Lee Strasberg Theater & Film Institute, Bowery Poetry Club, Living Theater, etc. (NYC); California Institute of the Arts and Beyond Baroque Literary Arts Center (LA); Wesleyan University (CT); University of Colorado (Boulder); McGill University (Montreal); Catholic University of America (Washington, DC); Cite des Arts and University of Louisiana, (Lafayette, LA); October Gallery (London, UK); Trinity and Saint Peter's Colleges, University of Oxford (Oxford, UK); MES International Theater Festival (Sarajevo, Bosnia Herzegovina); the SIBIU International Theater Festival (Sibiu, Romania); and more.

Allan often collaborates with artists, performs his works and that of other writers widely, and lives in Manhattan.

LAY OUT YOUR UNREST

www.ingramcontent.com/pod-product-compliance
Lightning Source LLC
Chambersburg PA
CBHW041142170626
46815CB00007B/343